Small Words:
Volume 1

by

Mark Smith

for A.

Birds

Blossom Haiku

In the camouflage of leaves,
 Watching and Waiting,
  Iridescent eyes of Love

The Gathering

The gathering of the birds begins like the outbreak of spring rain, imperceptibly, in small groups of twos or fives.

The groupings merge to a Cloud, a Miel, or a Murmuration, into a visible, vibrating brush-stroke of sky. Half-chaos, part-epic, a living organism, both pulsing and flowing, flashing on-off-on, from colour to shadow, from order to fury, and back again, like light that is both particle and wave.

Occasionally, single specks will be thrown clear, or misjudge the moment's turn or sudden twist. Yet gravity will not let them loose, soon draws them back, without collision, urgency or demand.

The Birds weave, dive and soar, individually, and in soundless harmony, as if drawn by some unseen hand, by avian conditioning, social ritual or the sheer unfettered pleasure of flight.

Earth-bound, we stare, as mesmerised and uncomprehending, as upon strangers in love. We see all we are and nothing at all, and all things we cannot be, and all else between.

Peregrine

Peregrine had been the leader for as long as anyone could remember. He was like a father to them all, even though he had no offspring of his own. Through many generations of hatchlings, through the seasons of greening, fruiting and browning, he had watched over them.

When he was younger, he had dreamed of such a life and, even though it was widely acknowledged that his display was by far the most numerous, it failed to charm, lacking the spectacular opulence and iridescence of his kind: its acknowledged quality being strangely muted, with fine grades from the dark blue of the moonlit sky, to the mottled greens of the deep pond.

Over the years the pain of loneliness had slowly subsided as he learned to take pleasure in the communal success of the group.

One day, mid-August, near the low hedge to the side of the formal garden, while feeling too weary and too contemplative even to forage, Peregrine was disturbed by a gentle rustling, a singular snapping of twigs in the undergrowth. Before him were eyes as deep and sensitive as his own, her feathers seemed to shimmer amongst the leaves, between shade and warmth.

Peregrine felt a change in the seasoned timbre of his heart until, in a startling burst of scattered leaves, smoke and fire, she was gone...

Heart

Five Years

Five years ago today, my heart came to me in a dream and said:

"We are tired. We have been hurled into the sky and left to fall on stony ground. Dragons have set us aflame with their fierce breath. The silence of Four Winds have torn at us from every direction and scattered us to every corner of our known world. We have been drowned in rivers of rage and been lost across seven seas of tears. Bonfires have burnt us to cinders and drawn despair from our own dust. We have been made brittle by the betrayal of ice and the unkindness of frost. We are tired. We wish to be as strong as oak. We wish to grow and feel the sun upon us."

In my dream, my heart began to sprout roots, forcing through arteries, deep into muscle, carving into my bones, reaching every nerve in my hands, my feet, my head. A thicket twinned around me again and again. The thicket became a trunk around my chest, as solid as teak, my legs became roots reaching to the centre of the world; my arms and hair became branches holding the sun in the azure sky above my head.

From the branches came verdant leaves and delicate fronds, and from the leaves came flowers of subtle shades and diverse colours, and deep amongst the dense comforting foliage, I saw the weave and thread of the only place I could call home, and deeper still the camouflage of plumage, and from the darkness, her iridescent eyes that spoke of nothing, and of everything, and of love.

Leaves

It is when I see the aerial display of spinning sycamore leaves, or spiky horse chestnut cases scattered and broken open on the ground beneath an avenue of wind-snapped branches, that I am reminded of our childhood and those times, in darkening and frosty autumns, when there was still enough warmth in the sunshine to rush around in the woods and gardens in only our sweaters, free from the heavy constrictions of our winter overcoats, and of how we used to dance amongst piles of leaves, kicking them high into the air and watch them take flight again; or how we would gather them into deep beds, up to our knees and beyond, then hurl ourselves into the crispy, crunching cushion; or bundle them into great fistfuls, to cast them exuberantly above us like giant balloons and watch them explode in the wind.

As the days grew shorter, we would watch the leaves flush like rosy-cheeked Heritage apples, or deepen to a scabby Pippin crimson, or wither to delicate silver, and of our wonder at their lacy decay, as if woven by spiders.

Then here we are, nearly fifty years later, and I think of you and the leaves in my heart that scatter like darting sparrows and startled starlings and, in the background, the sound of our laughter.

Weave

One day, in Spring I think, my icy heart dissolved into a million snowflakes. From an avalanche of pain, I fled, from shame and fear, deep into the dank darkness of the forest.

I crafted myself a new one, from the leaves I had gathered from my foraging, woven together with spruce needles and knot-weed; leaves from the dry ash, the smoky oak, and the flighty sycamore; or stripped from the bitter birch, whipping willow and the poisonous yew; from elm, beech and hornbeam. Chestnut, bramble and holly were also used to add texture, flavour and contrast.

It was a glorious patchwork treasure of diverse colours; from aged smoky grey to a green of sap-filled youth; a dry-blood crimson to the blue-veined cheese of my grandfather's hands; silvers from gun to moon, and mercury; tans of sand, old leather and burnt umber; colours that brought to mind fresh-cut grass, late-year sunsets, and yellow-bruised purples; a visible kaleidoscope of Technicolor wonder. For those who could see it, it was truly an object of desire and beauty, almost good enough to devour.

Then, one day, in Autumn I believe, my heart caught fire...

Tree

Evergreen

Roots
are where it begins,
tell us everything we need
to know, and make us who we are.
They hold us firm against the everyday howling winds.
The sturdy trunk bonds us to the land, building a plinth
for branches that stretch their arms to reach for
the sun, and the buds that foretell of change,
of leaf, of blossom, and of fruit.
The leaves are our voice,
quivering with laughter,
and singing out our joy.
Throughout the
very longest
of nights,
these will
not shrivel
or curl or
fall. For,
like life,
like love,
like memories, in happiness, they remain evergreen.

Lone Tree

The tree was ancient, almost as old as the earth beneath his roots. He had seen a great forest of friends cut down in their prime, as The Travellers pushed their way through the knot-weed and bracken, then chopped, cleared, and finally scraped the ground before them. His friends became cabins and fences, his family became furniture and wagons, until he alone stood.

What seemed to be a daily occurrence to him spanned the changing yearly landscape. Hundreds of years of life altered beyond recognition in a single sweep of the sun. The arid smoke, every blackening fire, all the familiar cries, each bit into his bark, soaked into his sap, and poisoned his heart to its roots, yet through it all, he survived.

He thought his time would soon come, he dwelt on his likely demise, as the years passed on the wind. He felt sure he would meet his end as a coffin in the earth, or shipwrecked on the fabled sea beyond the horizon, but the little people never came for him.

Town Tree

The other day, while walking to the centre of the small coastal town where I live, across its hillside streets, near the battle-gaming park and bowling club, I noticed the familiar hop-step-jump of a Magpie, carrying in its beak, a branch broken by the recent strong overnight Spring-tide winds, some two and a half or three times its own wingspan, and marvelled how the bird struggled to hoist itself into the air, due to the imbalance of its cargo, from ground to wall to fence to branch, then away and how, as we were walking hand-in-hand through your town, a few hours later, came the realisation that, amongst the dirty chaos splattered concrete paving, against the rowdy churning diesel of the local buses, amidst the sparse, consumptive trees in the main shopping area, and the cawing of crows from three raggedy woven nests, that your hand gently resting in the space between collar and neck, or your head nestling in the hollow beneath my collarbone would be a place as close as I have ever know to call home.

Well

Well-Loved

It was while I was recording the migratory progression of the so-called Kilmartin-Bell effect on the lichen of western Scotland, on behalf of a now-obscure foundation, that I encountered an elderly man of Gaelic ancestry and whose name, as he sonorously gargled its vowels, reminded me of a character from the later works of Flann O'Brien, and whose weathered complexion resembled the granite stonewalling of the surrounding sheep-cotes, and whose verdant eyes were flecked with the same mischievous glint of grey quartz, as he told me how he first met his recently-deceased wife, and how, as a young man nearly a century earlier, he had saved the young maiden, the last in her village, from being sacrificed to a hideous Grendel that dwelt at the bottom of the well in the nearby village, by continually showering small stones and large pebbles into the deep darkness for forty days and forty nights until, driven to madness and despair and no longer able to contain his rage, the ogre appeared at the well-head just as he, the boy, swung his axe, before remarking how, like gods, even monsters can be made to forget themselves.

The Well

The River was everything to the villagers, though they gave it no name. Their village nestled in its protective loops and curls, as if in a lover's nightly embrace. It asked nothing from them for itself.

The Town Well was purposely placed at its centre. It was the heart of their lives. It was here where they would gather as a meeting place, to celebrate feast days, announce news, welcome guests, honour feats and where they came to solve disputes amongst them.

On market days, they would circulate about it, regardless of the season, like children staying close to a beloved and protective parent.

Its waters nurtured their crops in spring, refreshed them in the heat of summer, it fed them in the winter in their soups and stews.

One day, The Authorities came and demanded to know the name of their place. The Villagers gathered together at The Well and it was there they decided that the name of their place was Love.

The Dig

The Miners came to the place the Diviner had chosen, high on a hill, surrounded by a circle of trees. They knew it would be exhausting work but began with cheerful diligence, cutting away thick spadefuls of grass and earth, in a clockwise spiral of steps. It was slow progress through a moraine of shale, and almost stalled at a stubborn, thigh-deep layer of bedrock, had it not been for the Diviner's zeal and encouragement.

The further they dug, the more the dangers became apparent to the men; the fear of collapse, the falling of debris. One was struck on the head; another fell from exhaustion; the weariest of men became ill. Eventually, heavy supports were required and the excavated rocks were used to line the core of earthwork.

They laboured, deeper and deeper, stripped to vests and shorts, while their numbers continued to dwindle. The air became sour and dank; the men grew irritable with one another and fights were common; some passed out and, when recovered, they too departed. Fresh food and water became scarcer, never knowing whether it would arrive from one day to the next.

In the dark, one miner grew petrified of disturbing the Grendels that were said to live there; the others laughed. More left until, finally, the last remained. He could hear the tip-tap of heavy steps ascending on the ladders. He continued alone as the walls grew hot and humid, as if he had reached the earth's centre, resting little as the daylight became a single star point of light until, as both strength and hope began to desert him, he cut through the last of it and found what they had all come there seeking.

Lightning Source UK Ltd.
Milton Keynes UK
UKHW040740100822
407113UK00002B/579